this book belongs to:

CDW

SUPERHERO FOR A DAY

THE **MAGIC** MAGIC EIGHT BALL

DUSTIN BRADY

ISBN: 1537238175
ISBN-13: 978-1537238173

CONTENTS

ACKNOWLEDGMENTS

Special thanks to Jesse Brady for the cover and interior illustrations. You can check out more of Jesse's sweet artwork on Instagram: @jessnetic.

CHAPTER ONE
STUPID ON THE INTERNET

"There's nothing wrong with crying if it hurts."

"It doesn't hurt, so why would I cry?"

It did hurt. Very much. But Jared Foreman was determined not to show pain on video.

"Just a few more seconds. You can do it, buddy."

Kodey Kline, the kid behind the camera, was not Jared's buddy. Kodey was in sixth grade like Jared, but he had the chin hair of a high schooler. In James Ford Rhodes Middle School, that was enough to make him a man among boys. Kodey mostly used his power to get people to do dumb things that he could then record and post online. He was the one who had challenged Jared to this particular feat of strength —

attempting the splits while people stacked books in his arms.

"Five! Four! Three! Two! One!" Kodey led the small crowd surrounding Jared in a countdown. "Woohoo! You did it buddy!" He tussled Jared's hair and walked away.

"Hey!" Jared yelled. "Someone get these books!"

Although a few people stuck around to stare and snicker, nobody came to get the books. Finally, Jared had no choice but to tip over and let the books fall everywhere. He stood up, wiped himself off and started cleaning up. Another set of hands came to help him.

"Oh," Jared said when he noticed. "Hey Bre."

Breanna Burris was the coolest girl in sixth grade,

or at least Jared thought so. She wasn't a "cool" cool girl — she didn't hang out with the popular crowd or take a million selfies or anything. But she was funny and athletic and always happy and, again, Jared just thought she was the coolest.

"You OK?" she asked.

"Oh, yeah. Yeah for sure." Jared said, trying to hide the fact that his face had started turning red. "Kodey just told me to — we thought it would be funny if I did the splits while holding a bunch of books. And it *was* funny! I mean, I haven't seen the video yet, but I think he's gonna put it up later..."

"Well I'm glad you're OK," Bre said with a smile as she picked up the last book. "Wouldn't want your pants splitting in half."

"Hahaha!" Jared overlaughed while she walked away. "No we wouldn't!" He smiled stupidly in her direction.

"You done fooling around?"

Jared spun around. His cousin, Lenny Patterson, was standing behind him with an impatient look on his face. Jared walked home from school with Lenny every day, and every day Lenny was late for some dumb reason. One day he would be trying to clean a giant ink stain from his pants, another the nurse would be testing him for a concussion after he had hit himself in the head with his own locker, another he would —well, you get the idea. Lenny would be fine waiting this one time.

"I wasn't fooling around."

"Yeah, you were too busy looking stupid for the Internet," Lenny said.

"No, it was funny."

"For everyone else. I don't know why you let him do that to you."

"Do what?" Jared asked. "Kodey's a friend."

"Whatever that guy is, he is not your friend. Would a friend leave you with all those books?"

"He didn't hear me ask for help."

"And that thing last week, would a real friend dare you to eat a booger? Someone else's booger? And would a real friend trick you into calling the teacher "mom"? And would a real friend…"

Lenny spent the walk home recounting all the ways in the last month that Kodey had maybe not been a real friend. By the time they reached the park where they split off to their own houses, Jared had had enough.

"You're just jealous that Bre was hanging out with me."

Lenny squinted at him. "Just now? For like two seconds?"

"I would say ten to fifteen seconds."

"Because she felt sorry for you?"

"What? No! Come on. She thought it was funny too."

Lenny jumped and grabbed a branch above his head. He started swinging himself back and forth "Whatever you've gotta tell yourself."

Jared didn't know why this conversation was making him so mad, but it was, so he did something to make himself feel better. He pushed Lenny. It wasn't that hard of a push — it shouldn't have done anything — but since Lenny was not the most coordinated of sixth graders and since Jared got him on the upswing, Lenny fell directly onto his back and got the wind knocked out of him.

Jared crouched down to check on his cousin. "Are you OK? I'm really sorry, I didn't mean to do that."

This would usually be the time for Lenny to retaliate with a punch to the stomach. Instead, he lay staring at the tree he had just fallen from. "What's that?"

Jared followed his gaze to a small crevice in the base of the tree. Deep inside, tucked away so that it was only visible to someone lying on the ground, was something that looked round, black and plastic. Jared walked over and reached his hand into the hole until he felt it. Even though it was plastic, it gave him a small zap of static electricity when he touched it.

Jared pulled out the object and examined it. It was a black, oversized billiards eight ball with a small window on the back. Inside the window was a blue triangle that read, "DON'T COUNT ON IT."

"What's this?"

"You've never seen one of those before?" Lenny said as he sat up. "That's a magic eight ball."

"How does it work?"

"There's a dice thingy inside with different answers on every side. You ask a yes-or-no question, shake the ball real good, and the dice thing floats up to the window with your answer."

"Oh brother."

"See if it works. Ask it if Bre just 'hung out with you' because she felt sorry for you."

Jared rolled his eyes.

"Do it."

Jared sighed, held the magic eight ball to his mouth and asked, "Was Bre just feeling sorry for me?" He shook the ball, waited a second and got his answer.

YES, DEFINITELY

Lenny laughed as he turned toward his house. "Told you. See you tomorrow."

Jared stood glaring at the eight ball in his hands. "Why would she feel sorry for me? I don't believe you."

He sighed and started walking home. After a few seconds, he glanced back down and stopped dead in his tracks. The magic eight ball had a different message now. One that did not seem to answer a yes-or-no question. One that seemed very, very specific to his particular situation.

BECAUSE YOU LOOKED STUPID ON THE INTERNET

CHAPTER TWO

THE MAGIC MAGIC EIGHT BALL

Jared's heart started pounding. "Who are you talking about?"

BREANNA BURRIS

Oh boy. Ohhhhhhhh boy.

"Lenny! LENNY!!" Lenny was already out of earshot. Jared suddenly became aware of the empty park around him. Had anyone else seen? He stuffed the magic eight ball into his book bag and ran home. His mom caught him as he burst through the door.

"Hey hon, how was school?"

"Fine! Good! Great!" He ran past the snack on the table and up to his room.

"Hey!" Jared's mom called up to him. "What's wrong with you?"

Jared didn't even turn around as he ran up the stairs. "Lotta homework tonight, Mom! LOTTA homework!"

As soon as he closed the door, he tore open his book bag and started firing questions at the magic eight ball.

"When is my birthday?"

JANUARY 4

"What time is it now?"

3:37 P.M.

"What will the weather be tomorrow?"

PARTLY SUNNY WITH A STRONG THUNDERSTORM AT 3:10 P.M.

"Who will win the World Series this year?"

CLEVELAND INDIANS

Jared got an idea. He opened his math workbook and turned to the day's assignment.

"What's the answer to question 1?"

3 3/8 INCHES

Question 2?

2.7 KILOMETERS

Within two minutes, Jared had finished all his homework. He picked up the phone and called Lenny.

"Lenny! You've got to come over now!"

"What's wrong? Why are you out of breath?"

"You know that eight ball we found?"

"Yeah."

"It's magic!"

"Uh, yeah. It's called a magic eight ball."

"NO!" Jared was now screaming into the phone and hyperventilating at the same time. "IT'S A MAGIC MAGIC EIGHT BALL!"

"I don't understand."

"IT KNOWS EVERYTHING! Just come now!"

Lenny sighed. "Did your mom buy more of those peanut butter-stuffed pretzels?"

"What?!"

"Do you guys have those peanut butter-stuffed pretzels I like?"

"That's not important right now!"

"It is important, because I'm only coming over if I can eat peanut butter-stuffed pretzels."

"DO WE HAVE PEANUT BUTTER-STUFFED PRETZELS?!" Jared asked the eight ball.

YES. THAT WAS YOUR SNACK.

"They're on the table. NOW COME!"

"On my way." Lenny hung up.

Jared held the eight ball up to his face. It felt like he had some sort of superpower. He got right to work using it. A few minutes later, he heard the front door open.

"Hi Aunt Mary!" It was Lenny. "Oooooh, are these peanut butter-stuffed pretzels? Are you sure? Thank you!" Lenny walked into Jared's bedroom with a bowl of peanut butter pretzel pillows.

"OK," he said with a full mouth. "Let's see it."

Jared held out a deck of cards. "Think of one."

"I thought you were…"

"Just think of a card!"

"OK, got it."

"What is it?"

"Six of hearts."

"Reach into the bottom of your bowl."

Lenny dug around in the bowl and pulled out a six of hearts. Jared waited for his jaw to drop to the floor. It did not.

"Uh, OK. You do magic now? I thought you said the eight ball was magic."

"Think of another card."

"Okay, but…"

"You were thinking of the five of diamonds."

"What are you…"

"Think of another one."

"How did you…"

"King of spades. Think of another."

"Jared…"

"Seven of clubs. Do another."

"JARED!"

"What?"

Lenny had gone a little pale. "What is going on?"

Jared smiled. "Was I right?"

"Yes. Every time. How are you doing that?"

Jared held up the magic eight ball. "I asked it before you came over."

"What do you mean you asked it?"

"I mean I asked what cards you would think of when you walked in here, then I hid the first one in the pretzels."

"But that's just a toy. It doesn't answer real questions."

"What color underwear are you wearing today, Lenny?"

"I'm not answering that!"

Jared showed the eight ball to Lenny.

GREEN WITH BROWN BEARS

Lenny turned red. "For your information, they're ninja bears!"

"I don't know how it knows, but it knows everything."

"I want to try! I'm the one who found it anyways." Lenny grabbed the eight ball. "What is 47 times 38?"

VERY DOUBTFUL

"Give me that." Jared took the eight ball back. "What is 47 times 38?"

1,786

"Why is it only working for you?"

"Who knows."

"And why does it work in the first place?"

"Who knows."

"And shouldn't we tell someone about it?"

"You want to risk getting it taken away?"

Lenny shrugged. "I don't know, I mean it's not ours, right?"

"And who does it belong to then? An elf? It was inside a tree."

"Ask it."

"What? No."

"It knows everything, right? Ask it who it belongs to."

Jared huffed and mumbled, "Who do you belong to?"

He shook the eight ball, looked at the answer and gasped. He showed it to Lenny. There was the jaw hitting the floor reaction Jared had been expecting all along.

JARED FOREMAN

CHAPTER THREE

WINNER WINNER CHICKEN DINNER

"It's mine! It's mine it's mine it's mine it's mine!" Jared did the magic eight ball dance around his room — a dance that consisted mostly of hideous disco moves.

"What are you going to do with it?" Lenny asked.

"I have some ideas. Let's go!" Jared started walking out the door.

"Wait," Lenny said. "How long are we going to be? I've got to study for tomorrow."

Jared rolled his eyes. "Really? Are you really going to be like this?" He held up the eight ball. "Is Mrs. Harness going to cancel the history quiz tomorrow?"

YES

"See? She always cancels quizzes on Friday. Now let's go!"

Lenny shrugged and followed Jared downstairs. Jared's mom caught them on their way out the door. "Where are you two off to? I was just starting dinner."

"We're going to the library to work on a big history project," Jared said without breaking stride. "We'll eat at Lenny's."

Jared's mom gave them a weird look. Lenny avoided eye contact.

"OK, just be home at a reasonable hour."

"For sure Aunt Mary, we…" Jared grabbed Lenny by the collar and led him out the door before he could blow it. The cousins hopped onto their bikes, and Jared led the way right past the library to the carnival that was in town for the weekend. They locked up their bikes and wandered to the midway, which was just gearing up for the night with flashing lights and goldfish in bags and funnel cakes as far as the eye could see. "You ready to win some gigantic stuffed bears?" Jared asked.

Lenny shrugged. "We need tickets to play the games, right? I didn't bring any money to buy tickets."

"We don't need money when we have this." Jared held up the magic eight ball. He smiled and whispered to the eight ball, "Where can we find a ticket that somebody dropped?"

LAST PORTA-POTTY ON THE RIGHT

Jared and Lenny walked down the long line of porta-potties and opened the green one at the end. Sure enough, underneath a piece of toilet paper in the corner was a crumpled, red ticket. Lenny wrinkled his nose, but Jared picked it up. "Where else?"

Underneath the Ferris wheel. Inside the funhouse. A bunch in the parking lot. Within 15 minutes, Jared and Lenny had found $50 in forgotten tickets. By the time they had uncovered the last ticket from a glob of nacho cheese, Lenny was all in. "Where to first?!"

"There." Jared pointed to a green stuffed gorilla the size of a Great Dane. It was hanging over ring toss — the game where you have to throw a small ring over the mouth of a glass bottle.

"That game's impossible," Lenny said.

Jared wiggled his eyebrows. "We'll find out."

The ring toss guy, who looked like he'd spent too many years running this game and had maybe slept in the ring toss booth last night, sprang to life when Jared walked up. "Thereyago young man, thereyago, fifty rings for just five tickets, fifffty rings, put a ring on any bottle and win any prize, any prize you see here, step right up, step right up, step right up."

Jared forked over five tickets, making sure to get rid of the gross porta-potty one first. After getting his bucket of rings, he stared at the sea of bottles in front of him. How would this work with the guy right there? Just then, a high school couple walked by, and the ring toss guy got distracted. "Ohhhhhh, she has her eye on a stuffed dog, did you see that young man? Did you see it? Win her love by winning man's best friend, just five tickets for fifty rings, five tickets for fifffffffty…"

While he was making his sales pitch, Jared broke out the magic eight ball. "Where should I aim?"

BETWEEN THE BLUE GORILLA'S EYES

Jared looked at Lenny and shrugged. Instead of aiming for one of the bottles in front of him, Jared located the blue stuffed gorilla hanging ten feet above the game. He closed one eye, squinted with the other and tossed his ring between the big ape's eyes.

The ring smacked the gorilla's forehead, slid down its nose and fell onto the bottle below.

CLANG!

The worker spun around to see his first ring toss

winner in three weeks.

"Winner winner chicken dinner!" Lenny yelled.

"You can't lean over the counter," the worker said.

"I didn't!" Jared yelped. "I hit it fair and square!"

"You leaned over the counter. I saw you."

"He didn't, I was a witness!" Lenny said.

"I don't think he did," the teenage girl piped up.

The carnival worker turned to her and glared.

"It's OK," Jared said as he took another ring. He aimed again, and again he hit the gorilla between the eyes.

CLANG!

The ring fell onto the same bottle and rested on top of his first ring. Ring toss guy looked like he might be sick.

"I'll take the green gorilla!" Jared said.

The worker handed him the gorilla. "Nice shot kid. Have a good day." He started to reach for Jared's bucket of rings.

"Wait, I've got 48 more rings!"

The guy looked like he might argue, but instead

shrugged and turned away.

"Hey," the teenage guy yelled. "I want to try this game!" While the teenager bought his rings, Jared went back to the magic eight ball.

"What next?"

SKIP THE RING OFF THE COUNTER

Jared took a step back and aimed at the counter like he was skipping rocks in a pond. This was a bit more difficult — he threw the first two rings a little wobbly, and they missed the mark entirely. But on the third try...

CLANG!

Ring toss guy slowly turned around.

Jared grinned. "I'll take the dog."

The worker handed him the dog and shooed him away. "You're done here, kid."

Lenny stepped up. "Can I try?"

"Five tickets."

"But we've got 45 rings left!"

"Five tickets."

Lenny harrumphed and handed over five crumpled tickets. Ring toss guy handed back Jared's bucket.

"Don't I get five more rings?!"

The worker ignored him and turned away. Lenny turned to Jared. "What do I do?"

Jared didn't answer right away. He was trying to figure out if the eight ball was just messing with him now.

"Hello," Lenny said. "I want to win a SpongeBob SquarePants big enough to be a mattress."

"Uh, it says to throw it at his head."

"Whose head? His head?!" Lenny pointed at the worker who was angrily talking on the phone with his back turned. Jared nodded.

Lenny smiled. "With pleasure." He took aim and threw the ring like a Frisbee at the baldest spot on the guy's head.

CLANG!

The guy spun around with steam coming out of his ears. "WHAT THE..."

Lenny and Jared stood pointing to the ring that had bounced from the guy's head onto a nearby bottle.

"BOTH OF YOU! OUT!"

"But we..."

"OUT!"

Jared and Lenny grabbed their prizes and shuffled away. On his way past the couple, Jared handed his dog to the girl.

"Awwwwww, really?!" the girl squealed and hugged Jared. He turned a little red and smiled at Lenny. Before the worker could jump over the counter and chase them away, Jared whispered something into the teenage guy's ear. He winked and walked away. A few seconds later, Jared heard the...

CLANG!

:...Of another winner and the...

"AHHHHHHH!"

...Of a carnival worker losing his mind.

CHAPTER FOUR

MICKEY MOUSE

Jared rolled over in bed and looked at the magic eight ball tucked into the covers next to him. "Was that all a dream?"

NOPE

Wow. What a night. After ring toss, Jared and Lenny won big at darts and the fishing game and that one where someone tries to guess your birthday. They ate pizza and giant turkey legs and so many elephant ears that Jared felt like he was going to puke. Then they rode the Zipper until Lenny did puke. They wrapped up the night by winning even more midway games. By the time they were ready to leave, they had put together a mountain of prizes so big that the local paper took a picture of them. Jared couldn't risk alerting his parents by bringing his prizes home, so now the shed behind Lenny's house was bursting with oversized stuffed animals.

Jared stretched and jumped out of bed. Today

was going to be a great day. He had big plans for school. First he called Lenny.

"Mrff?"

"Hey Lenny! How good of a mattress was SpongeBob?"

"Mmmmmfffff."

"Cool. Hey, you know that enormous octopus we won? Can you bring it to school today? Oh, and can you get there early?"

"Mmmhmmf."

"Thanks buddy!"

Now to put things in motion. He turned to the magic eight ball. "What's Kodey's locker combination?"

An hour and a half later, Lenny joined Jared in front of the lockers. "You really think this is going to work?"

"Come on, I ran it all past the eight ball. Did you turn that note into the office?"

"Yeah I did. But, hey, I was just thinking — this all seems a little over the top, don't you think?"

"Was eating 10 pounds of elephant ears a little over the top?"

"Yeah, probably."

"But didn't that make last night the best night of your life?"

"I mean, it made me throw up…"

"I'm just trying to make today as much fun for us as last night was."

"Uh OK, it just seems like a bad idea to make him mad. Also, it kind of feels like you're showing off."

"Yeah sure whatever," Jared mumbled as he kept his eyes down the hallway. "Oh, there he is!" Jared took his iPod Touch out of his pocket, pointed it at Kodey and started recording.

Kodey gave him a weird look as he walked down the hallway. "What are you doing?"

"Just filming my day at school, that's all."

"OK weirdo, just point that somewhere else."

"Sure thing!" Jared said as he pointed it at Kodey's locker.

"Weirdo," Kodey mumbled. He stepped up to the locker. 3. 27. 17. Click…

KAPOW!

A giant stuffed sea creature sprang from Kodey's locker.

"AHHHH!" Kodey screamed a high-pitch scream. He stumbled backward until his back foot stepped onto a skateboard that someone had carelessly left on the ground, almost as if that person knew exactly where Kodey would be stepping. Kodey's foot zoomed backward until...

RRRRIIIIIIIP

...He did the splits. The perfect splits. Splits so perfect that his pants ripped in the back, revealing Mickey Mouse undies. The crowd that had gathered when they heard the scream gasped at the underwear, then let out a roar of laughter.

Kodey's face turned bright red from embarrassment, then, when he saw Jared still filming with the iPod, dark red from anger.

"You!" He marched toward Jared. "You did this!"

"Did what?"

Kodey grabbed Jared and lunged for his iPod. "I'm going to shove this down your throat!"

Jared knew the lunge was coming, so just before Kodey could reach, he tossed the iPod over his head into his left hand. Kodey lunged again. Jared dropped it onto his foot and kicked it back into his right hand.

"AHHHHH!" Kodey lunged a third time. Jared

tossed the iPod high into the air.

"Hey! HEY!" Vice Principal Fuqua pushed through the crowd. Mr. Fuqua marched the march of a man who had spent a decade in the Special Forces. He didn't of course — he was bony and nearsighted and hadn't served a single minute in the military. He REALLY enjoyed military history, however, and was constantly acting like he lived in one of those black and white war movies. Right now, he was coming at Jared and Kodey with the pent-up fury of a man who hadn't handed out a detention in days. "What's going on here?!" Mr. Fuqua shouted. When he said, "here," he gestured toward Jared and Kodey. And when he gestured with his hand, Jared's iPod fell directly into his palm.

"He was trying to take my iPod, sir," Jared said.

"He sabotaged me!"

"Sir, I didn't do anything. The whole thing's recorded on that iPod you're holding. You can skip to the end if you want to see."

Mr. Fuqua swiped his finger on the iPod. "I'm going to shove this down your throat!" Kodey yelled from the tiny speakers.

Mr. Fuqua pointed at Kodey. "After school detention." Kodey threw up his hands and turned back to his locker. That's when Mr. Fuqua noticed his Mickey Mouse Clubhouse briefs. "You have a change of clothes, son?"

Jared piped up. "I have an extra pair of pants he can borrow, sir."

Mr. Fuqua nodded. "Thank you. We all good here?"

Jared nodded. Kodey huffed.

"Very good." Mr. Fuqua handed the iPod back to Jared and walked away.

Jared turned to his locker and handed Kodey a plastic bag. Kodey got real close to Jared and snatched it. "We're not done," he snarled before marching to the bathroom to change.

Jared barely heard the threat. He was too busy grinning like an idiot at Bre four lockers away.

"You OK?" she asked.

"Yeah, great! Do you want to see the video?"

"I can't believe you recorded the whole thing!" Bre said as she walked to class with Jared. As they walked past Lenny, Jared gave his cousin a thumbs up. Lenny shook his head.

The bell rang a few minutes later, and Mrs. Pierce started class. "Let's begin by collecting last night's math homework. Make sure you…"

Kodey walked into the class.

"…Oh. Oh my. Mr. Kline, that is quite a fashion statement."

The class giggled. Kodey's new pants were checkered white and bright blue, and they flared into two huge bell bottoms. Jared grinned. The magic eight ball was right again — the pants fit perfectly.

CHAPTER FIVE
MAGICAL TREETOP HIDEOUT

A huge group gathered in front of the lockers after class. In the middle of it all stood Jared Foreman, telling the future.

"You're going to get an 85 on the science test Monday."

"What about me? What about me?"

"Uhhhh, 59. I'm so sorry."

"How are you doing this!"

"It's a gift."

"Jared! Jared!"

Next to him, looking on in amazement, was Bre Burris.

"I'm sorry guys, I'll try to get to everyone. If you don't get your future this morning, I'll be back in the afternoon, where for a small fee…"

Lenny pushed through the crowd. "Jared, can I

have a word?"

"Not now, Lenny."

Lenny pulled him aside anyways. "You need to stop."

"I need to stop helping people?"

"I don't know that telling people what they're going to get on a test is 'helping' them. I also don't think that you'll get to keep your little ball for too much longer if you keep showing off for the whole school."

Jared put his hand on Lenny's shoulder. "I'm sorry you're so jealous."

"What?! Why would I be jealous?"

Jared tilted his head toward Breanna. Lenny squinted at him. Jared sighed and snuck the eight ball out of his book bag. "Is Bre still hanging out with me because she feels sorry for me?"

NO.

He held up the answer for Lenny, then winked a very annoying wink and turned back to his fans. "Sorry everyone. My cousin over there is just upset that I found out he wears teddy bear undies."

The crowd roared its approval. Lenny turned red and marched away.

"Hey Bre," Jared whispered to Breanna. "Want to see something cool?"

"Now?"

"Sure, why not?"

"Cuz we have to go to class."

"We're already excused from it. Follow me."

Jared led Breanna through the school to a door marked "Maintenance Only." He pushed open the door, walked up a dark staircase, and opened another door at the top.

"Isn't this cool?"

They found themselves on the roof of the school, surrounded by a dome of overhanging tree branches with leaves turning every shade of orange, yellow and red. The way the morning sun was hitting the trees made the colors breathtaking. Jared felt like he'd been transported to a magical treetop hideout.

"Whooaaaaa," Bre marveled. "This is amazing! I love the fall."

"I know," Jared said.

She gave him a sideways look. "You know?"

"Oh, uh, yeah. Everyone loves the fall!"

Bre turned back to the scene in front of her and smiled again. Then she frowned. "What did you mean that we were 'already excused?'"

"Earlier this morning, Lenny turned a note into the office saying that the three of us were excused from science and history to help set up for the school drama. He was supposed to join us up here, but I think he's a little cranky right now."

Bre made a face. "Set up for the drama? Do you think that's really going to work?"

"I *know* it's going to work."

"You sure know a lot of stuff today."

Jared grinned. This was the best day.

Bre took one more look around and turned toward the door. "This was really cool, but I think I want to go back to class now."

"Wait, wait!" Jared stopped her. "I have one more thing to show you."

"What?"

"The back exit." With that, Jared took off toward the edge of the roof. Ten feet, five feet, one more step, and suddenly he was flying through the air, doing a perfect cannonball off the school.

"JARED!" Bre screamed. She ran to the edge and looked over. There was Jared, lying on a stack of wrestling mats piled ten feet high.

"Haha, isn't that cool?!" Jared yelled up. "You try!"

"I — I can't," she said. "I'm scared of heights. I'll just, uh, I'll take the stairs."

Bre disappeared from the roof, and Jared closed his eyes. That could have gone better. He opened his eyes again, hopped off his tower of mats and started dragging them back to the gym.

"Excuse me."

Jared jumped. He wasn't expecting anyone — the magic eight ball had specifically said that he wouldn't get in trouble.

"Are you Jared Foreman?"

Jared turned around. Standing behind him was a tall blond woman holding a microphone and newspaper. She had the paper opened to the community section and was pointing to the picture of Jared and Lenny posing like goofballs on top of their prize mountain.

"Yes, that's me."

"Hi!" The woman smiled a TV smile and held out her hand. "I'm Emily Spivney with Channel 5 News! How are you?"

"Uh, pretty good."

"This picture is incredible!" she said. "We thought it would be fun to do a story for the seven o'clock news about how you won so many prizes. Would that be OK?"

Jared thought about it. On one hand, his parents would definitely find out that he'd fibbed about the library once they saw him on TV. On the other hand, they'd probably find out eventually since the picture made it into the paper. Plus, how many people get to be on the news?

"OK!" Jared said.

"Great, follow me!" Emily led Jared to a Channel 5 News van parked in front of the school. "Do you know where Lenny Patterson is?"

"He should be in Mrs. Harness's history class."

"OK! I'll grab him real quick." She motioned to the open back door of the van. "You can wait in there and check out the equipment if you want."

Jared peeked into the news van. It was filled with tons of computers and blinking electronics. "OK, cool!" He climbed in and moved a laptop from one of the benches.

"Great!" Emily said. "Be right back."

Jared looked around at the van. He had tried to act cool around the news lady, but he couldn't contain his glee by himself here in the van. He let out a weird giggle. Not even 24 hours ago, he was the one people were making fun of. Now, he was going to be on the news. The news! Bre would be so impressed.

Uh oh. Bre. Jared had forgotten that she was on her way down from the roof. Any second, she'd reach the mats and think that Jared had ditched her. Did he have enough time to find her and come back before the news lady returned with Lenny? He pulled out the magic eight ball.

"How long until Lenny shows up?"

An answer appeared behind the glass. Jared felt a stab of fear in his stomach. It wasn't the answer he was expecting.

He nervously looked around the van, then jumped out of his seat to make a break for the open door. As soon as he stood up, however, the van roared to life and lurched forward. The sudden movement caught Jared by surprise, and he fell to the floor, dropping the eight ball in the process. As the van took off, the eight ball rolled out the door and onto the street. Before Jared could struggle to his feet again, the van screeched to a sudden stop, slamming the back door closed. Then it sped off, carrying Jared farther and farther away from his precious eight ball.

The eight ball rolled to a stop next to the curb, still displaying the one-word message that had turned Jared's world upside-down:

RUN!

CHAPTER SIX
AN OCEAN OF DOO-DOO

Locked.

Back door. Side door. The little window to the front seat. All locked. Jared looked around for something he could use to escape or contact the news station. Upon closer inspection, he found that the equipment in the van — high zoom lenses, long-distance microphones and what seemed to be remote listening devices — looked more like they belonged to a spy organization than Channel 5 News. Jared panicked and banged on the side of the van.

"Help! HELLLLLLLLLP!"

The van never slowed. It flew around corners, knocking Jared around his prison cell like a pinball. After just a few minutes of driving, though, it stopped. The engine shut off, and Jared heard the sound of someone jumping out of the van and crunching gravel under their feet as they walked around to the back.

Uh oh.

The footsteps stopped and waited. A minute later, Jared heard the sound of another set of feet running up to the van. Finally, the back door opened. The sudden light made Jared squint. He could see that the van had parked in a secluded spot in the woods — probably the woods next to the school. Two people stood outside: the blond news lady from before, out of breath like she had just run to the van, and a short, muscular man with a camera. Jared cowered in the corner.

"Sorry about that," News Lady said as she climbed into the van and fixed her hair. "We got kicked out of our parking space in front of the school, so we had to move."

Camera Guy followed behind her and closed the door.

"Do you mind if we ask you a few questions before we go on camera?" News Lady continued. "It's kind of a pre-interview we always do."

Jared looked around the van. "Uhhhhh, I think I want to go back to school."

News Lady smiled. "Of course! This will only take a few minutes. We just wanted to find out how you won so many prizes last night."

"I, uh, I got really lucky I guess."

News Lady raised her eyebrows and turned to Camera Guy. "Really lucky? Wow, I wish I had luck like that! Right Jim? Hahaha!"

Jim did not laugh.

She turned back to Jared. "Jared, please don't be modest. Surely you've got some secret you could share with our audience. We're not going to be able to air this segment if you don't give us anything."

"I'm really sorry. I don't know what to say."

She sighed. "It's OK. I understand. Lenny must be the one with all the carnival skills, right? We'll just have to track him down."

Jared suddenly felt very sick. "Wait! No! It was me! It was all me! Don't get Lenny, please don't get Lenny!"

News Lady and Camera Guy looked at each other. "OK Jared," News Lady said. "If you say so. But you'll have to tell us something."

"OK, I, well, I have to think about it, uhhhh, you see…"

Camera Guy sighed and shook his head. News Lady took that as her cue to tighten the screws a little bit.

"Jared, I'm going to be honest with you. We know you had some extra help last night. We just need to know what it was."

Jared looked back and forth at the two of them. "Do you guys work for the carnival?"

This got a huge laugh from News Lady. Even Camera Guy cracked a little smile.

"Because if you do, I'm so sorry. I was just…"

News Lady interrupted.

"You really think the carnival is going to send a $3 million van to find out what happened to a few little stuffed animals?"

"I mean they were pretty big stuffed animals, but…"

"Jared," News Lady got closer. "Here's what I think. I think you've stepped into a pile of doo-doo, and you have no idea how big it is. Well let me tell you, it is big."

"Like how big?"

"Like an ocean of doo-doo."

Jared gulped.

"So let me keep you from putting yourself or anyone else in danger. What. Happened. Last. Night."

"OK OK OK, I'll tell you everything."

But Jared didn't get a chance to tell them everything. Because at that moment, the back door flew open and something hit Camera Guy in the back of the head. He roared and held his head.

"JARED! RUN!"

It was a girl's voice. A familiar girl's voice. She screamed again.

"RUN!"

It was Bre.

CHAPTER SEVEN
JUNK CITY

Jared used the moment of distraction to roll between Camera Guy's legs. On his way out the door, he saw the object that Bre had thrown at his captor — the magic eight ball. He grabbed it and plopped gracelessly to the ground.

"LET'S GO!" Bre grabbed his arm and started running into the woods. "FIND OUT WHAT WE NEED TO DO!"

"How should I…"

"I KNOW ABOUT THE EIGHT BALL, JUST ASK IT!"

"Where do (gasp) we go?" Jared asked the eight ball while trying to run and catch his breath at the same time.

LEFT

Jared and Bre stumbled left. They heard Camera Guy and News Lady jump out of the van behind them. "Now what?!"

DOWN THE RAVINE

Jared looked at the ravine to his right and swallowed hard. It was super steep. He made it exactly one step before tumbling all the way to the bottom. He cleared his head and turned back to see Bre riding down the hill, using fallen leaves as a snowboard while yelling at him.

"GO! GO! GO!"

Jared got up and led the way along the bottom of the ravine while the news people followed parallel at the top. Jared continued asking the eight ball for their next moves, and it continued to deliver — even if some of the moves seemed really weird.

PICK THE PLANT ON YOUR LEFT

DUCK UNDER THE LOG

TAKE THE PATH ON YOUR RIGHT

GRAB THE SHARP STICK

RUN FASTER

Jared and Bre ran along the path until they emerged from the woods into the part of downtown known as "Junction City." Jared had been to this neighborhood many times — his mom loved it, and his dad was fond of calling it "Junk City." It consisted of restored buildings from the 1800s, where shop owners would sell fancy candles, overpriced antiques and popcorn with gross stuff in it.

TO THE FIREHOUSE

Jared and Bre ran into Firehouse Fudge, a candy store inside of the old fire station. It was just opening for the day. When they stepped inside, bells on the door jangled and a cat sleeping in the sun jumped from its spot.

"Be right there!" the shop owner called from the back.

BE QUIET

Jared motioned for Bre to shush.

GIVE THE CAT YOUR PLANT

Jared handed the cat the small weed he had picked in the woods. When the cat smelled the plant, its eyes lit up, and it started rolling on its back like crazy. It batted the plant, and in the process, batted the bells some more.

"I'm coming, I'm coming!"

HIDE BEHIND THE COUNTER

A gray-haired woman emerged from the back, looked around the store and noticed the cat.

"Whiskers! How did you find the catnip?"

While she took the plant away from the cat, Jared and Bre snuck into the back room and up the old staircase to the firehouse roof. From the roof, Bre could see News Lady and Camera Guy. They were sprinting through town, looking around corners and inside of shops. "I think we're safe for now, Jared," she said.

But Jared wasn't paying attention. He was too busy firing questions at the magic eight ball.

"Jared? We're just going to hide up here for a while, right?"

"Nope," Jared said as he untied one end of the rope from the flagpole on top of the firehouse and unlooped it a few times.

"Why not?!"

"Because if they can't find us, they're going to go after Lenny. We can't let them go after Lenny."

"So what's the plan?"

Jared remained silent until he finished tying the rope around the stick he'd taken from the woods. "This," he said as he walked to the edge of the building. "HEY!" he called out.

News Lady and Camera Guy, who were crossing the street again, looked up.

"UP HERE!"

They bolted for the firehouse.

Bre pushed Jared. "What's wrong with you?!"

"It's all part of the plan," he said before throwing the stick like a javelin as hard as he could. The rope was just long enough to reach the store across the street (Sandy's Sassy Scarves 'n' Such in the old courthouse), where it looped around the bell tower. Jared grinned at Bre. "See! It's a zipline!"

Bre pushed him again. "I literally just told you that I hate heights!"

"Oh, uh, I forgot about that."

Bre got right in his face and held up her finger. "You are the WORST person to protect."

"To what?"

She didn't answer. Instead, she took off her jacket, looped it over the rope, squeezed her eyes shut and jumped.

"AHHHHHHHHHHH!"

Jared did the same with his belt. As the eight ball predicted, they both made it safely into the second-story window of the courthouse. Also as predicted, a police car pulled up in the middle of the street to check on the ruckus.

"They're after us, and they have guns!" Jared yelled to the officer.

"Who's after you?"

"THEM!"

Jared pointed to News Lady and Camera Guy, who had reached the firehouse roof.

"You two! Stop!" the officer shouted at them.

They didn't hear him. They were too busy mounting the zipline — the hastily made zipline that to this point had been fortunate to hold two skinny sixth graders.

RRRRRRRRRRRIP!

Sure enough, the line snapped from the firehouse as soon as both of the thugs put their weight on it. News Lady screamed and hung onto the rope as it swung them…

THUNK!

…Smack onto the police car. The officer cuffed them both as they struggled.

"That. Was. Awesome!" Jared said as he turned to give Bre a high five.

She ignored the high five and walked to the opposite side of the building.

"You think that's it?" she asked as she opened the window and hopped onto the fire escape staircase outside. "Thanks to you, it's just the start."

CHAPTER EIGHT
SUPERHERO FOR A DAY

"The start of what?" Jared asked as he followed Bre onto the fire escape.

"What time is it?" Bre asked.

"I don't have a watch."

Bre rolled her eyes and turned around. "You have an eight ball that tells you everything you could ever want to know! JUST ASK IT!"

"OK, OK. I keep forgetting. No need to get huffy. What time is it?"

11:08 A.M.

Great," Bre said. "And what time did you get the eight ball?"

"I don't know, like 3:30?"

"Wonderful. You've wasted almost 20 hours."

"I haven't understood a word you've said for the past five minutes."

"Of course you haven't. Just follow me and make sure nobody sees us."

Bre led Jared back to the woods. She turned off the path, avoided some prickly vines and found a single boulder near the creek. She put her shoulder against the boulder and pushed until it moved a bit, revealing a big hole underneath. She motioned to the hole. "After you."

Jared slipped into a shallow cave. Bre followed, then covered the hole with something before turning on an electric lantern in the corner. The space lit up to reveal a cave the size of a bedroom with rugs on the floor. One side of the cave had beanbag chairs, and the other was lined with crates filled with comic books — lots and lots of comic books. There was Spider-Man and Wonder Woman and the Fantastic Four and a million others all neatly organized into color-coded crates.

Jared whistled and walked toward the comic books. "Cooooooooool."

"Don't touch anything!" Breanna said.

Jared spun around. "What's wrong with you? You're always like the happiest girl in school, and you were being super-duper nice to me this morning."

"Yeah, because I was undercover!"

"WHAT ARE YOU TALKING ABOUT!"

"Why don't you ask your little eight ball?"

Jared looked down.

BRE WAS SUPPOSED TO GET THE EIGHT BALL

Jared looked back at Bre, more confused than ever.

She sighed, plopped down on a beanbag chair and started talking. "Last year, I found a note in my locker. It said, 'Do you want to be a superhero for a day? Circle YES or NO.' I thought it was a weird joke, but of course I circled YES, because — just in case, you know? The next morning, the note in my locker was gone. In its place was a pair of white sneakers. They were completely plain except for the Spider-Man motto printed under the tongue."

"What's the Spider-Man motto?"

"With great power comes great responsibility."

"Oh."

"Anyways, I put the sneakers on and found that they let me run fast. Like super fast. Like supersonic. I could run so fast that time seemed to stand still. That day, I ran to California and back. I jumped across the Grand Canyon. At the end of the day, I even found out that I could walk on water."

"Sounds pretty awesome."

"It was very awesome. I ended up falling asleep at like 3 a.m. with the shoes on. When I woke up the next morning, they were gone. They'd disappeared. That's when I understood — superhero for a day. I turned on the TV to find out if any of my adventures made the news. What I saw instead was the Hamilton Hotel fire. Remember the Hamilton fire downtown last spring? Remember all those people trapped on the sixth floor?"

"Bre..."

"Remember those firefighters who kept running up and down stairs to get people until it was too late?"

"Bre..."

Bre's eyes started getting watery as she talked faster. "Remember those five people who didn't get rescued in time? One was a first-grader named Jackson. He had a big cowlick and three teeth missing in that picture they showed of him on the news. Do you remember that? Because I remember it every day."

"Bre, come on. You can't think that you're somehow responsible for what happened to them."

"With great power comes great responsibility. I had great power. So yeah. I was responsible. But I was too busy having my own fun to notice anyone else around me."

Jared looked down. The cave was silent for a bit.

After a few seconds, Bre collected herself and continued. "I got another note in my locker that morning. 'Don't feel bad. We all have to learn this lesson. I'm truly sorry you learned it the hard way.' That's all it said. A few weeks later on the first day of summer vacation, I found a gift addressed to me on the front porch. It was a pair of X-Ray glasses that really worked! I put them on and ran all over town, trying to figure out how to use them to help people. We had record high temperatures that day, do you remember?"

"Mmmhmmm," Jared said, even though he didn't remember in the slightest.

"By the end of the day, I was soaked in sweat and no closer to helping anyone than I was when I left that morning. But at 5 o'clock, when I was ready to go home, I saw something move in a car as I walked through the Kroger parking lot. I looked closer and saw that someone had forgotten a baby in the backseat. The car's windows were tinted — nobody else could have seen the baby. I ran as fast as I could into the store and got help. The store manager broke the car window and someone else called 911. The paramedics who came told me that I'd found the baby just in time."

"That's so cool!"

"Probably six or seven times since then, I've gotten another superpower for a day. Always a day — exactly 24 hours."

"Why 24 hours?"

Bre shrugged. "I've been reading a lot of comic books lately to learn about the best ways to use different superpowers. It seems like most people with superpowers either turn bad or become miserable. Superpowers that last for only 24 hours let you do something great without getting into a lot of the trouble that comes with being a superhero."

"And you don't know who's giving you these notes?"

Bre shook her head. "No clue. Anyways, the superpower always comes just in time to stop something awful, and it always comes in the form of something that looks normal — a baseball hat, a squirt gun, a jar of Silly Putty."

Jared started putting the pieces together. "Uhhh, or perhaps a magic eight ball?"

"Yeah. Perhaps a magic eight ball."

"Oh boy."

"My note yesterday morning said that I would find a magic eight ball inside a tree at the park on my way home from school that I could use to stop something bad."

"Well if the eight ball's yours, can't you just use it now?"

Bre shook her head. "The superpower only works for the person who touches it first. Probably for protection in case they get captured. When you picked it up, you felt a tingle, right?"

Jared nodded.

"That was the eight ball starting the 24-hour timer. So after you got the superpower, my new job was to protect you from yourself so you didn't do anything stupid."

"That's why you were hanging around me so much this morning?"

"Until you decided to jump off a building."

"Sorry about that."

"I didn't realize you'd already done something stupid last night by getting your face in the paper as the carnival king."

"Oh."

"I'm not the only superhero, you know. Others are popping up too, and criminals are starting to figure it out. So they're on high alert for anything suspicious — like someone who can win enough carnival games to build a mountain of stuffed animals."

"But we got the bad guys arrested, right? Isn't everything fine now?"

"No everything is definitely not fine! Once they figure out the first two goons got arrested, they'll send more! That's why we're staying safe in here for the rest of the day."

Although Jared definitely wouldn't mind spending the rest of the day in the Batcave, something was bugging him. "You said that you were supposed to use the magic eight ball to learn about something bad that was going to happen, right? Can't we still do that?"

"Too dangerous with people looking for you."

"But they're still going to be looking for me after the superpower goes away, right? Isn't our best bet stopping them while the eight ball still works?"

Bre thought about it for a second. Jared tried to help by showing her the magic eight ball's answer.

YES

Bre sighed. "Well you made things real hard for us by wasting so much time and bringing so much attention to yourself."

"Then we need to get going! Did your note say where to start? Maybe like a mobster hideout or mad scientist lair or something."

"Yeah, it did say actually." Bre uncovered the hole again, and light streamed into the cave. "The school lunchroom."

CHAPTER NINE
GRANDMA MURRAY

Jared followed Bre out of the cave. "The lunchroom? Really? What could possibly be going on in the lunchroom? I mean that meatloaf is a crime, am I right? Hahaha."

Bre rolled her eyes in the most exaggerated way possible. "Can you just help me push this rock back into place?"

Jared put his shoulder against the rock and pushed. "And can we just talk about this magic eight ball for a second?" he asked. "Like, how does it know what's going to happen?"

"I don't know, but these things are never actually magic. My guess is there's a tiny supercomputer in there that figures out what's going to happen. The note said that it performs some light time travel calculations."

"Light time travel? What does that even mean?"

"Light time travel! Like a small amount of time travel — I don't know, I'm just telling you what the note said."

"And we're using this powerful, time-traveling computer to uncover a lunchroom plot?"

Bre pointed to the eight ball. Jared looked down.

YUP

Bre stopped Jared when they could see the school through the trees. "We've got to be careful," she said. "You said those passes that Lenny turned in are only good through the morning, right?"

"Well yeah, but can't we just tell someone that there's an evil plot inside the lunchroom?"

"Do you want to be the one to tell them that we discovered this plot from a magic eight ball?"

"Oh. Probably not."

"Just stay low and keep out of sight."

The eight ball led Jared and Bre to the back delivery entrance. They waited the one minute and 46 seconds the eight ball said it would take for the UPS guy to walk through with a package, then scrambled inside right before the door closed all the way. The eight ball led them around two hall monitors to the school kitchen. Jared paused to consult the eight ball again, then slowly opened the kitchen door.

None of the lunch ladies noticed two sixth graders in the kitchen because they were too busy with the early lunch rush. Jared and Bre crawled inside the pantry and peeked around the corner. Jared prepared himself to see something truly horrific — like the hot dogs being made from real dogs. What he saw instead was definitely worse.

Nothing.

Nothing exciting was happening. Just bored adults doing boring adult things. Jared waited for a minute before looking back down at his eight ball and whispering, "What are we looking for?"

JUST WAIT

Another minute later, one of the lunch ladies walked back to the pantry. It was Grandma Murray — Jared's favorite because she would always scoop out extra pudding. Grandma Murray wasn't actually a grandma to anyone in the school, but all the kids called her "grandma" because she had gray hair and remembered everyone's birthday. Bre and Jared shrank behind a stack of paper towels while Grandma Murry rounded the corner.

"I'm sorry!" she shouted over her shoulder. "I told

my doctor that lunch is the worst time for appointments, but he never listens!" She turned back to the pantry, flipped on the light, nervously looked around and started loading bread onto a cart.

Stealing bread? Seriously? It wasn't even the good bread. She was taking the gross gluten-free bread the school kept for kids with wheat allergies. Grandma Murray looked around again before wheeling the cart out the door. Jared turned to Bre.

"Are all of your adventures this exciting?"

"Just ask it what to do next."

Jared rolled his eyes and asked.

FOLLOW HER

"Let's go!" Jared whispered with mock excitement. "Maybe she's stealing jelly too!"

Bre sighed. "Come on."

Jared led the way out of the kitchen. He walked with the confidence of someone who knew his biggest danger came from a grandma stealing bread. This was unfortunate, because just then an actual danger spotted him.

"Hey Buttface."

Jared turned to see a pair of plaid bellbottoms walking toward him.

"Hey Kodey."

"Give me that iPod."

"I don't have time for this right now."

Kodey stepped so close that his chin hairs could almost touch Jared's nose.

"I said give me that iPod."

Bre piped up. "We don't have time for this."

That caught Kodey off guard for a second. He turned to Bre. "You two the dynamic duo now?" He sneered. "Cute. Real cute. Well I'm sorry to break up this date, but..." He spun around clocked Jared in the jaw. When Jared stumbled backward, Kodey lunged for the pocket where he'd seen Jared put the iPod that morning. Instead he pulled out the magic eight ball.

"Give that back!" Jared yelled as he lunged at Kodey.

Kodey held the eight ball high above his head and smiled. "Should I give it back?" he asked the magic eight ball.

MY SOURCES SAY NO

"Ohhhhhh," Kodey stuck his lip out in a pouty face. "So sorry, my sources say no. But if you want, you can..."

POW!

Bre landed a karate kick to Kodey's face.

"Owwwww!" Kodey stumbled backward and dropped the eight ball. Jared scooped it up and started running.

"What is going on?!" Vice Principal Fuqua heard the commotion from down the hall and started walking toward Jared and Kodey.

"What is going on?" Jared repeated the question. "Well, I…" he looked down at the eight ball for help.

RUN

Jared put his head down and booked it toward the service exit. Bre followed close behind.

"Hey! STOP!" Vice Principal Fuqua yelled. Jared didn't stop. He was now a fugitive from school, which didn't feel great. When he burst through the service door with Bre, he spotted Grandma Murray loading the last of the bread into her minivan.

"Follow me!" Bre yelled. Jared followed Bre to the side of the school where her bright pink bike was locked up. "Hop on!"

Jared wrinkled his nose and tried to come up with an excuse for not riding a girl bike. "Can this even fit two people? And like, do you have enough helmets…"

"HOP ON!"

After witnessing that karate kick one minute earlier, Jared decided that arguing with Bre might not be smart. He sat on the seat. Bre straddled the bar in front of him and started pedaling.

"There she is!" Jared pointed to a minivan turning left onto the street. Bre put her head down and pushed harder. Fortunately, Grandma Murray drove like — well — like a grandma, so Bre could keep up just enough to spot the van before it made its next turn. Even more fortunately, the drive lasted only three minutes. Bre made it to the last street just in time to see Grandma Murray turn into a factory with a sign out front that said "Allied Fresh, Inc."

"Do you think that's it?" Jared asked.

Bre didn't answer. She was staring at something in silence. Jared followed her stare to a van parked in the shadows next to the factory.

It was the news van from earlier.

CHAPTER TEN
DON'T BE A BABY

"I changed my mind," Jared said.

"Cool," Bre said. "You want me to drop you off back at the school then? Cuz I'm sure they're real excited to talk to you."

"Oh, uh, I mean…"

"Come on, you're a hero now. Don't be a baby."

Bre and Jared hid the bike (as much as one can hide a hot pink bike in the grungy factory part of town) and crouch-walked to the side of the building. Grandma Murray was just finishing unloading the bread from her van onto a cart. They hid as she walked past them into the door.

"Now what?" Jared asked the eight ball.

TO THE ROOF

Bre shook her head. "Why does it always have to be the roof?"

Jared asked the eight ball a few more questions and led Bre back to the news van. "It says we have to climb on top of there and then make the long jump onto that awning, where we'll roll..."

Bre closed her eyes. "Stop. I can't think about it or I'll throw up. Just lead the way, and I'll follow."

Jared shrugged, jumped onto the hood of the van, then completed the *American Ninja Warrior* course the eight ball had laid out for him to get to the roof. Bre followed step for step, making sure to never look down. When they got to the roof, Bre let out a long sigh. "We made it! Now where?"

THE AIR VENT

"Seriously?!"

Bre walked to the air vent and stared in disbelief. Jared joined her. "Well," he said. "I agree that it doesn't look like the sturdiest..."

"It's an AIR vent! It's made for moving air! Not people!"

"Well yeah, but in the movies, people always crawl through air vents."

"THIS IS NOT THE MOVIES!"

Bre had a point. Jared asked the eight ball again. Again it came back with the air vent. "Are you sure?"

he asked. "Because I don't think this will hold…"

DON'T BE A BABY

"I just decided that I don't like that thing," Bre said.

Jared crawled in first, then Bre. The air duct was pitch black and filled with spider webs. The words on the eight ball glowed a little bit, so Jared put the ball face-up in his shirt pocket to use as a little flashlight as he crawled forward. He made it just a few feet before hearing a loud *creeeeeeeeeeaaaaaak*. He paused. Bre held her breath. Jared crawled one step forward and then —

SNAP!

His stomach flipped into his chest as the air duct dropped a couple of feet. He tried to hold on, but the duct had turned into a slide. Bre rolled into him, and they both tumbled down the duct and crashed through the ceiling into a closet filled with empty boxes. They didn't have time to check for injuries, because they heard an adult voice as soon as they landed on the boxes.

"What was that?!"

They got low. The voice was coming from the next room. A walkie talkie beeped.

"Greg," the voice said. "Check the roof. Sounds

like something crashed up there."

"Got it," another voice crackled over the radio.

Jared looked around the room. A little bit of light was streaming in through a vent near the ceiling. He stacked up boxes to climb and get a better look. Bre joined him. The vent was just big enough to let them peek into the office next door, where they saw a tall, bald man towering over Grandma Murray. The middle-aged man was wearing a lab coat and looked perfectly normal except for his left hand. His left hand was twice the size of his right and seemed to be covered in a sort of tree bark.

"I just need you to promise me that this is safe," she said.

The bald guy put his right hand (the normal one) on her shoulder. "Of course, Mrs. Murray. You're doing something good here."

"Because it doesn't feel good."

"Mrs. Murray, not only are you earning enough money to send your niece to college," he patted the briefcase on the desk, "but you're also an important part of research that will change millions of lives."

"If this is so good, I don't understand why I have to sneak around."

"Mrs. Murray, as I explained earlier, this is for

science. People are always going to try to stand in the way of science. Like the true pioneers of science before us, we must do whatever is necessary to make the world a better place. Do you understand?"

Grandma Murray sighed. "Not really, but just as long as it's safe for the kids."

"Of course it's safe. Now if you'll excuse me, I'd like to make sure that everything is progressing well. The bread should be ready to take back to the school any minute now."

Grandma Murray nodded, and the guy walked out of the room.

FOLLOW HIM

Jared cracked open the closet door to find that they'd landed in an office area overlooking the factory. The bald guy walked down the stairs, while Jared and Bre hung back in the shadows on the catwalk above. They watched the bald guy talk to some factory workers below, then pick up one of the loaves Grandma Murray had brought. He opened it, sniffed it then nodded approvingly.

"What are they doing?" Jared whispered.

LOOK BELOW

Jared and Bre looked down. Directly below them, two factory workers were tearing open loaves of the school's gluten-free bread and dunking them slice-by-slice into an open bag filled with white powder. They would then dust off each piece of bread, weigh it on a scale, dust it some more, and put it back into the bag.

Jared turned to Bre and shrugged. None of this made sense. It certainly didn't seem like an operation that would require thugs in vans scaring kids. What were they missing?

Suddenly Bre's eyes got big. She grabbed Jared's shoulder and pointed to the bag below. Jared squinted to make out the lettering. Wheat...wheat something? Then he saw it.

"100% WHEAT CONCENTRATE"

That didn't seem good.

He leaned over the railing to get a better look at the fine print on the bag. When he did, the eight ball fell from his shirt pocket into the open bag below.

That didn't seem good at all.

CHAPTER ELEVEN
CLUNK

DON'T LEAN

The eight ball, which had landed face-up in the wheat concentrate, was displaying a message that would have been real helpful for Jared to see seconds earlier. Fortunately, wheat concentrate is soft, so the ball's fall got muffled enough that nobody seemed to notice. Unfortunately, Jared was stuck in enemy territory without a superpower.

Jared turned to Bre, but she had already disappeared back into the closet. Jared followed her. In the closet, Bre furiously rummaged through junk.

"What are you doing?"

"Not so loud!"

Jared lowered his voice. "What are you doing?"

"We've got to get that eight ball back."

"No duh."

"Listen, can you just help me find... AHA!" Bre pulled out a long, thick rope from the pile of junk.

"What's that for?"

"I don't think we can take the stairs because they're out in the open. Our best bet is going to be this rope."

Jared had been hoping for something a little better. "You want to swing down like Tarzan?! That's your plan?"

"*I* don't want to swing anywhere. You're going to do it. Also, it's going to be a little more Spider-Man than Tarzan."

"What are you going to be doing during all of this? Planning my funeral arrangements?"

"I'll handle the distraction so nobody sees a sixth grader hanging from a rope in the middle of their factory."

"This seems less than ideal."

It took some convincing, but Jared finally came around to Bre's plan. She would take boxes into the ceiling, crawl to the opposite side of the factory, open up another ceiling tile and dump the boxes one by one onto the floor 30 feet below. While the workers would be trying to figure out what was going on, Jared would loop the rope around the railing to use as a pulley, then lower himself to the ground undetected. Bre would crawl back to the roof, and Jared would escape with the eight ball and bag of wheat to take to the police. As they say in the movies, the plan was so crazy that it just might work.

Jared helped Bre push a few boxes into the ceiling. He then found his spot on the catwalk, looped the rope around the railing and waited for his signal.

CLUNK!

That was it — the sound of a box hitting the ground. Jared took a deep breath.

A radio below squawked to life. "Greg, do you want to check that out?"

"I'm on it."

Without looking down, Jared looped his legs around the left side of the rope and started lowering himself to the ground with the right side. All the while, he heard Bre continue with her distraction.

CLUNK! CLUNK! CLUNK!

Just a few more feet.

CLUNKCLUNKCLUNK CRAAAAAAASH!

Wow, that was loud! Bre must have dumped all the boxes at once. Jared finally made it to the ground.

Like everyone else in the area, the workers dunking the bread had run to the other side of the factory to check out the commotion. Jared unlooped the rope from the railing and ran to the bag of wheat concentrate. He put the eight ball in his pocket, rolled up the bag and picked it off the table. That's when he felt the hand on his shoulder. Not a regular hand — more like a giant Hulk hand.

Jared slowly turned around. The hand was attached to the bald guy who had been talking to Mrs. Murray. Behind him stood three guys in lab coats. Behind them stood a scowling, stocky man wearing a blue shirt with a tag that said, "Greg." He was holding onto a beat-up Bre.

Bald guy motioned to Jared with his finger. "You need to come with us."

CHAPTER TWELVE
THE BEEHIVE

The bad guys — Jared was pretty comfortable calling them "bad guys" at this point — led Jared and Bre to a small room off of the main factory. On the way, Jared was able to work his way back to Bre.

"I'm sorry," Bre whispered. "The ceiling broke."

"It broke?"

"Yeah, like I was throwing boxes down, and then I heard a *crack*, and then I fell."

"Are you OK?"

"I think so. The boxes broke my fall a little. I just can't put too much pressure on this ankle." Bre shot Jared a little glare. "I told you I hate heights."

"I know."

Once they were inside the room — which was bare except for two seats and an empty metal table — everyone else left except for Greg and the bald guy.

Jared tried to plan his next move. Unless this Greg goon left them alone in the room, Jared couldn't pull the eight ball out of his pocket without risking it getting taken away. Greg stood in a corner and the bald guy motioned to the chairs.

"Please. Sit."

"We'll stand," Jared said.

Greg walked over and pushed them both down into the chairs. OK, perhaps they would sit.

"Hi," the bald guy smiled. "My name is Dr. Raymond Plotke. I own the building that you've broken into."

"We'll leave now," Jared said.

Dr. Plotke smiled again. "I'm sure you would like to do that. And I would like to help you do that. I'm just going to need you to help me help you by answering a few questions first."

"Why don't YOU answer some questions!" Jared shot back. Jared didn't know where this sudden courage was coming from, but he was feeling pretty good about being the tough guy.

Dr. Plotke spread his hands. "Ask away."

Jared wasn't expecting this. "Oh, uh, well why are you stealing our school's bread?"

Dr. Plotke chuckled. "Is that why you came all this way? Oh my, I didn't know James Ford Rhodes Middle School took bread security so seriously! If you must know, I'm actually borrowing the bread. It will be back within the next half hour or so."

"But why?"

"We're actually working on a very important cure here, and your school is going to be a crucial part of it," Dr. Plotke said.

Jared scrunched up his face. "What are you talking about?"

Dr. Plotke held up his gnarled left hand. "See this?"

Jared looked away.

"I know it's difficult to look at, but this hand is the most important thing that has ever happened to me. Please. Look at it."

Jared and Bre looked awkwardly at the tree hand while the doctor stared at them like he wanted them to say something. "Uh, cool," Jared finally said.

Dr. Plotke smiled and launched into a story that he had clearly told a bazillion times. "As a child, I was horribly allergic to bees. I missed half a week of camp in third grade after I blew up like a balloon from a single bee sting. After that, I was so scared of bees that I barely ventured outside for years. I would lock myself in my bedroom for days on end and lose myself in my chemistry sets. Then one day in sixth grade, I climbed into the attic to look for some equipment my mom had put away. I grabbed a rafter to pull myself up and suddenly felt my hand light on fire. I looked up to see that I'd grabbed a huge beehive."

Bre and Jared both winced.

"This hand," Dr. Plotke held up the tree hand, "was covered in bees — maybe 20 or 30. I fell backward out of the attic and ran into the kitchen, all while the bees stung me over and over. By the time I shook the last bee off, my hand didn't look like a hand anymore. I panicked and stumbled through the house looking for my EpiPen. Do you know what an EpiPen is?"

Jared shook his head. Bre spoke up. "It's like an emergency needle you can stick yourself with if you're allergic to something."

"That's right!" Dr. Plotke said. "I couldn't find my EpiPen. I called for my mother, but both my parents were gone. After a few minutes, I curled into a ball and passed out."

Both Bre and Jared had moved to the edge of their seats. "What happened next?" Jared asked.

Dr. Plotke whispered the next sentence like he was sharing the secret of the universe. "I was fine." He paused to let that sink in and smiled. "My mother woke me up when she got home and rushed me to the hospital. At the hospital, they took blood test after blood test. Finally, they told me that I was not only healed from the bee stings, but I was also no longer allergic to bees. The bees had cured me!"

Jared looked around the room skeptically. "I don't think that's the way it works. Maybe your mom gave you something while you were unconscious or the hospital gave you medicine or even…"

Dr. Plotke slammed his fist down. "IT WAS THE BEES! I DON'T CARE WHO GAVE ME WHAT, I'LL ALWAYS BELIEVE IT WAS THE BEES!"

"But what about your hand?"

"What about it? It works doesn't it?" Dr. Plotke flexed it a few times. "It's even better than my other hand because it doesn't feel pain."

Bre tried to change the conversation to settle the doctor down. "So what does any of this have to do with our school?"

"After that day, I felt like I could live again. I

didn't have to be afraid. In fact, every day since then, I've stung myself with bees to remind myself how it feels to be alive." He took a jar of bees out of his pocket like a real weirdo. Jared and Bre looked at each other uneasily.

"I want to give that feeling to others. That's why I've been working on my new wheat allergy cure."

Jared didn't know what to expect when he walked into the room, but a wheat allergy cure was not in the top 1,000.

"Ever since the bees cured me of my allergy, I've believed that the best way to cure an allergy is with the thing that's causing it. The body will do amazing things in its fight for survival, you know."

"So you want to cure kids who are allergic to wheat by giving them wheat?" Bre asked.

"Not just wheat. Wheat concentrate. One hundred times the amount of wheat in a regular piece of bread."

Bre and Jared looked at each other with wide eyes. This guy was officially nuts. "That could be deadly, right?!" Jared finally asked.

"I believe it will cure them."

"What do you mean you 'believe'? Haven't you tested this?"

"This won't work on animals. I feel that there's something special about the way the human body fights for life that turns the disease into the cure."

OK, that's just lunacy. Jared started to panic. "So you have a crazy feeling that you're testing on kids?! What if they get really sick? What if they die?!"

Dr. Plotke was starting to get annoyed. "Would you rather be sick for a day or live in fear of bread for the rest of your life?"

Jared turned to Bre with a "can you believe this nutcase?" look. Bre continued staring straight ahead. Her face had gone totally white.

"Once I share the results of my experiment, the

world will be knocking down my door, begging me to cure them. Now," Dr. Plotke spread his hands. "I believe that I've been more than fair in answering your many follow-up questions. I hope you'll provide me with the same courtesy."

Jared wasn't listening to Dr. Plotke. He was staring at Bre. Something didn't look right about her. "Bre," Jared whispered. "Are you OK?"

She didn't answer. Dr. Plotke decided to move forward despite the little whisper conference taking place in front of him. He turned to Jared. "You had quite the evening at the carnival last night, didn't you? And then you escaped a maximum-security van. And now you're here. You sure get around, don't you?"

Jared avoided eye contact and shrugged.

"Now Jared, two of my finest employees are probably going to jail because of you, and I almost lost a $3 million vehicle. Even then, I told you my secret, didn't I? The least you can do is share yours."

Jared picked at his fingernails.

Dr. Plotke sighed and nodded at Greg. Greg started walking toward Jared. Jared sprang out of his seat and ran toward the door, but Greg crossed the room in two steps and snagged him by the collar.

Jared tried to fight, but Greg was too strong. In three seconds, he found what he was looking for.

Dr. Plotke let out a low whistle. "Is that a magic eight ball? I haven't seen one of those in what — 20 years?"

When he saw the eight ball's message, he stopped. Then he backed up.

"What is that?"

Jared took a look at the screen. He squinched his eyes. The message didn't make sense.

RECORDING SENT

CHAPTER THIRTEEN
EMERGENCY EXIT

Recording sent? That's not even an answer to a question. Jared was so confused.

"What is that thing?!" Dr. Plotke yelled.

"It's just…"

Dr. Plotke looked frazzled. "Why does it say that?! What recording? Was it recording just now?!"

Ohhhhhhhh. Wow! Now Jared understood what the eight ball was doing. He played along.

"This is a police surveillance device," Jared lied. Bre shot him a look, but he continued. "It recorded everything you just said and sent it to the authorities. They're on their way now."

Greg dropped the ball like it was made of lava. Dr. Plotke grabbed his head and walked around the room. "Why would you do that? WHY WOULD YOU DO THAT?"

Jared picked up the eight ball from the ground. "You shouldn't do weird experiments on kids."

Dr. Plotke wasn't listening. He pulled his phone out of his pocket while giving instructions to Greg. "We've got to move. Send the lunch lady away, take care of the kids and start loading up the vans."

"What do you mean, 'Take care of the kids?!'" Jared asked.

Nobody answered. Greg started pulling something out of his pocket. Jared looked down at the eight ball.

HE MEANS KILL YOU

"WAIT!" Jared shouted.

Nobody waited. Also, the "something" in Greg's pocket turned out to be a gun.

"WAIT!" Jared tried again. "I, uh, I…"

"…I'm allergic to wheat!" Bre interrupted.

That got Dr. Plotke's attention. He lowered his phone. "What's that?"

"I'm allergic to wheat," she said. "So you can use me for your experiment as long as you let him go."

The room went silent. Jared mouthed "What are you doing?" to Bre. She didn't respond. Instead, she kept her eyes on Dr. Plotke with her chin jutted out.

Dr. Plotke shuffled around the room for a few seconds. "How allergic?"

"One time, I broke out in hives just from smelling wheat."

Dr. Plotke bit his nails. Finally he nodded his head. "OK, fine," he said. "But we're going to have to speed up the process." He took a syringe out of his pocket.

"No!" Jared lunged for the doctor. Too late. Dr. Plotke stuck Bre with the needle and emptied the syringe. The whole thing was over in less than a second. Bre sucked in a sharp breath. She was trying to look brave, but her shaking gave her away.

"Put her in the van and get rid of him," Dr. Plotke said as he walked out the door.

Greg grabbed Bre with one hand and went for the gun again with the other. Jared looked at the eight ball.

RUN. HE'LL MISS.

Jared ran.

BANG!

Greg missed.

Jared rolled into the hallway.

TURN LEFT

Jared turned left.

TURN RIGHT

Jared turned right.

HIDE IN THIS ROOM

Jared dove into the room on his left. "Now what?"

STICK YOUR FOOT INTO THE HALLWAY

Really? Sometimes Jared didn't know about this thing. He took a moment to catch his breath, then stuck his leg into the hallway while trying to keep his body inside the room.

FARTHER

Jared sighed and pushed his leg out as far as he could without ripping his pants.

THUDTHUDTHUDTHUD!

Someone large was running toward Jared.

THUDTHUDTHUDTHUD!

He braced himself for impact.

THUDTHUD...

Jared felt a foot clip his leg.

"WHOA!"

THUNK!

Jared peeked into the hallway. One of the doctor's henchmen was lying on the floor, out cold. He'd tripped over Jared's leg and smacked his head on a cabinet. Jared scrambled to his feet.

EMERGENCY EXIT

Jared found the emergency exit at the end of the hallway and ran outside just in time to see Dr. Plotke and Greg load Bre into the news van at the other end of the building. Although it had only been a minute or two since Bre had been stuck with the syringe, she wasn't looking too good. Even from far away, Jared could tell that her face was getting puffy and her steps were shaky. Jared put his head down and ran toward the van. He didn't even stop to look at the eight ball. If he didn't get to the van before it left, he'd never...

VROOM!

The engine roared to life, and the van took off. Jared was left alone in an empty parking lot.

CHAPTER FOURTEEN
PATTON

"IS BRE OK?"

FOR NOW

"HOW LONG IS 'FOR NOW'?!"

UNTIL 3:44 P.M.

Jared needed help. Lots of help. Like, the Army would be nice. He ran to Bre's bike and took off toward the only help he could think of, which unfortunately also happened to be the place he'd run away from a few hours earlier.

His plan (if you could call it a plan) was to run into the school screaming. He hadn't quite worked out exactly what he'd scream yet, but he was pretty confident he'd figure it out in the moment. Once he got to the principal's office, he'd explain everything and lead police to Bre using the eight ball. "What time is it now?" he yelled as he pedaled.

1:27 P.M.

Jared had owned the eight ball for 22 hours now. During that time, he'd managed to tick off the school bully, embarrass his cousin, become a fugitive from school, get on the radar of some very bad people, and put an innocent girl in huge danger. He did win a stuffed gorilla though. Jared remembered the message Bre had received in her locker after the fire about "learning the hard way" and pedaled harder. He made it back to the school a few minutes later, dumped the hot pink bike in front of the doors and ran into the hallway.

"AHHH!" he screamed. It was not the most eloquent message, but it seemed to get the job done. People in classrooms peeked into the hall. He screamed louder. "AHHHHHHH!"

A hand grabbed him. "Gotcha!"

Jared looked up. Vice Principal Fuqua. "I'm so glad to see you!" Jared said. "I need to…"

"Save it!" Mr. Fuqua grabbed Jared by the collar and marched him toward the office. "You're in more trouble than any kid has been in ever! Cutting class. Fighting. Running away from school."

"I can explain everything," Jared interrupted. "You see, Breanna Burris is in trouble…"

"Oh she's definitely in trouble! Big time trouble!

But if you think you're pinning this whole thing on her, you've got another thing coming, mister!" Mr. Fuqua marched Jared into the school office with all the seriousness of someone who calls people "mister." They walked past Lenny, who was sitting in a chair with his arms folded. Even though Lenny saw Jared, he refused to do anything but glare at the ground.

Vice Principal Fuqua brought Jared into his office and slammed the door. "I'm going to be honest," he said. "You're probably going to jail. In all my years, I have never…"

Jared interrupted by pulling out the magic eight ball. "We don't have time," he said. "We need to use this to find Bre right now."

Mr. Fuqua snatched the eight ball out of Jared's hand. "What is this?"

"It's a MAGIC magic eight ball! It'll answer any question we ask! If you call the police, I can use it to lead them back to Bre. Please, you've got to trust me!"

Mr. Fuqua walked across the room, grabbed a piece of paper and came back to hold it in front of Jared's face. "Recognize this?"

Jared did recognize it. It was the fake note he'd had Lenny bring to the office to get him out of class earlier that day.

"You lost any chance for trust when you did this. I'm going to Principal Cochrane's office now, and together we're going to call both the police and your parents. Then we'll bring your cousin Leonard in, and — I'm only telling you this once — your stories had BETTER match up."

He marched out of the room with the eight ball. Then he locked the door from the outside, knocked on the door's window and taunted Jared with the key. After a few seconds of key wiggling, he disappeared into the principal's office.

Jared ran to the door and looked out the window. The secretary seemed to be on lunch break, so it was just Lenny sitting by himself in the school office. Jared knocked on the window to get his attention. Lenny wouldn't look up. Jared kept knocking, but Lenny had committed to ignoring him.

Jared frantically looked around the room for something he could use to communicate with Lenny. Vice Principal Fuqua kept a sparse office. Just a poster of the angry World War II general George Patton on the wall, a small bookshelf with a few books that had names like *Building Winners Not Weenies*, a simple desk with a laptop and a table with a weird printer/phone combination.

Maybe he could use the printer phone to call the police himself? But what if they didn't believe him either? Once Mr. Fuqua started arguing against him, they'd surely believe an adult over a kid who'd been doing nothing but lying all day.

Jared looked around the room again. He had to be missing something. Wait a second…that printer/phone thing! He'd seen something like it at his dad's work for "take your child to work day" last year. His dad had called it a — what was it again — a fax machine? It was supposed to send messages to people with paper and a phone instead of e-mail and the internet. Jared looked closer at the machine and found a list of numbers taped to the side. One of those numbers was labeled "SCHOOL OFFICE." He looked back out the window. Right next to Lenny's head was another fax machine. Jared got an idea.

He tore through Mr. Fuqua's office looking for a piece of paper. After a minute of searching, he decided that Mr. Fuqua must be the neatest neat freak on the planet, because his office didn't contain a single scrap of blank paper. He looked around one final time before taking a deep breath and ripping General Patton off the wall. He was already in more trouble than any kid ever, so why not pile it on? He scrawled a quick message on the back of the poster, fed it into the fax machine, dialed the number for the school office and hit "SEND."

A few seconds later, the printer next to Lenny came to life and spit out a piece of paper. Lenny continued glaring at the ground. Come on! Jared knocked on the window. Lenny kept glaring. Jared knocked harder. Lenny glared harder. Jared knocked and knocked and knocked until Lenny finally looked up, threw his hands into the air and mouthed, "What?!" Jared jabbed his finger at the printer. Lenny picked up the paper that had printed, gave it a weird look and turned it around to show Jared. General Patton. Jared had accidentally scanned the poster in front instead of his message on the back. He ran back, flipped the paper and scanned it again.

After a few moments, the fax machine next to Lenny printed another piece of paper. Lenny pulled it out, read it slowly and looked at Jared. Jared nodded. Lenny looked both ways, got out of his seat and walked to Jared. He got real close to the window. "What is this?" he whispered as he jabbed his finger at the faxed piece of paper.

It was a note that said, "I'M SORRY. I WAS WRONG. BRE'S IN TROUBLE. HELP!"

Jared tried to explain everything so Lenny could understand, but instead it came out in one jumbled sentence. "A weird scientist with bees and a tree hand gave Bre a wheat shot and put her in a news van and she might die!" he whispered with wide eyes.

"What?"

It took a couple more tries before Jared could get Lenny to half understand what had happened. Finally Lenny shook his head. "I don't know what you want me to do," he said.

"Please, you've got to help me get out of here so I can save her."

Lenny looked both ways and whispered a little louder. "Look, ever since that eight ball showed up, you've done nothing but get me into trouble. My mom is mad at me, your mom is mad at me, the carnival is probably mad at me, the school is DEFINITELY mad at me."

"I know," Jared said. "I was selfish, and I got you into a ton of trouble for no reason, and then on top of all that, I was mean to you, and I feel awful for how I treated you. I'm sorry."

Lenny sighed. Just then —

CLICK

Principal Cochrane's door unlocked.

CHAPTER FIFTEEN
CODE ORANGE

"Leonard, we're ready for you," Vice Principal Fuqua said as he stepped out of the office. "Leonard?"

Lenny was not sitting in his chair. Lenny was not standing in the office. Lenny was crouching in the corner behind a cardboard cutout of a little girl holding a box of cookies just out of sight of Mr. Fuqua. The vice principal looked around the office, then remembered the other troublemaker that he had locked up. "Jared! Jared, if you're a part of this, so help me…"

Mr. Fuqua looked into his office. No Jared. Also no Patton poster on the wall.

"JARED!" Mr. Fuqua unlocked his door and barged into the office. WHAT DID YOU…"

Jared spun out from behind the door and sprinted past Mr. Fuqua. He didn't have the eight ball to tell him if this would work, but he was hoping that

Lenny had remembered their move from Pee Wee football.

"COME BACK HERE!" Mr. Fuqua roared as he tried to grab Jared. "I'LL…"

THUNK!

Mr. Fuqua tripped over a balled-up Lenny lying on the ground. It was the same technique the cousins had used to get Jared his only touchdown of the season last year. When Mr. Fuqua tried to catch himself, he dropped the eight ball. Lenny scooped it up and joined Jared running out the door.

"I'M SO SORRY PLEASE DON'T BE MAD AT US!" Jared yelled on his way out. If his read face and roar of anger were any indication, Mr. Fuqua was not accepting the apology.

Lenny caught up to Jared. "Now where?"

Jared answered by diving into the school nurse's office. Fortunately, it was empty. "Where's the EpiPen?" he yelled once he got inside.

TOP DRAWER ON THE LEFT

Jared grabbed the EpiPen from the drawer while talking to the eight ball. "Should we call the police now?"

NO

"Why not?!"

THE BAD GUYS WILL LOCK THEMSELVES IN UNTIL IT'S TOO LATE FOR BRE

"So we have to sneak up on them?" Lenny asked.

"I guess," Jared said. "Where do we go?"

14346 LAKEVIEW DR.

"Lakeview Drive? My uncle lives there — that's the street on the lake with all those nice houses. It takes like a half hour to drive there!" Lenny said.

"How do we get there?" Jared asked the eight ball.

GRANDMA MURRAY

"I thought you said she was bad," Lenny said.

Jared shrugged. "I guess we've got to take our chances."

Lenny started opening the door, but Jared grabbed his arm. "Should we go now?" he asked the eight ball.

WAIT

Just then, the cousins heard the *CLOMP CLOMP CLOMP* of an angry vice principal running down the hallway.

NOW

Jared and Lenny ran the opposite way down the hallway toward the school kitchen. Inside the kitchen, they found Grandma Murray nervously scrubbing counters.

"Mrs. Murray, we need your help!" Jared panted as he rounded the corner.

Grandma Murray jumped when she heard the sixth graders. "You can't be in here!"

"We know about the crazy scientist!"

Grandma Murray dropped her sponge. "I—I said you can't…"

"Breanna Burris is in huge trouble right now because of that guy, but we can save her if we hurry."

Grandma Murray stumbled back a little and leaned against the sink. "I knew he was trouble. I knew it, I knew it, I knew it." She looked up at Jared and Lenny. "I didn't mean for anything bad to happen, I promise."

"It's OK Mrs. Murray," Jared said. "We just need your help."

Grandma Murray took a deep breath. "What do you need me to do?"

Just then an out-of-breath voice came over the school intercom. "Attention school. Attention school." (GASP GASP) "We have a Code Orange. This is not a drill." (GASP GASP) "Two fugitives by the names of…"

Jared looked at Grandma Murray. "First, it would be great if you could sneak us out of the school."

She nodded and directed the cousins to a metal cart. Lenny smooshed himself into the bottom of the cart and Jared tried to squeeze in after him. It didn't work. They tried several different combinations until they found one where both of them could fit into the cart if Jared curled into an upside-down ball. "OK, go!" Lenny said with his stomach sucked in.

Mrs. Murray put a tablecloth over the cart and started pushing it. "Oof!" The cart was a little heavy for her, but she pushed like a champ.

Squeak-squeak-squeak-squeak

If they continued at this pace, they'd reach the bad guys maybe next week.

Squeak-squeak-squeak-squeak

Maybe if Jared rowed with his hands a bit.

Squeak-squeak-squeak-CRASH!!

When Grandma Murray tried turning the corner into the hallway, she accidentally tipped the cart and dumped Jared and Lenny into the hallway. Jared tried scrambling back into the cart, but got interrupted by a swift kick to the ribs.

"OOF!" Jared crumpled to the ground. He winced and looked up to see a foot coming at him again. A foot attached to a pair of bright plaid bellbottoms.

CHAPTER SIXTEEN
REPLY HAZY

"OOF!" Another kick to the ribs.

Kodey sneered. "Too bad you don't have a girl to protect you this time."

"Wait!" Jared said. He grabbed his iPod out of his pocket. "You want this?"

"We are way past…"

"You can keep it."

Kodey stopped and stared at Jared.

"Let me just get it ready for you." Jared stood up and played with the iPod for a few seconds. "OK, it's yours." He flipped it to Kodey. "Enjoy."

Kodey looked down at his new iPod while Jared and Lenny took off toward the service exit. "I thought you were always going to give that iPod to me someday," Lenny said.

Jared winced with every step. "If you want to take

it back from Kodey, be my guest." The cousins crouched next to Grandma Murray's minivan and waited for her to emerge from the school. Jared glanced down and noticed Lenny's watch. "Hey Lenny, what time is it right now?"

"2:27."

"OK, first thing. Can you give me a heads up when it's almost 3:30?"

"Sure."

"Second thing. We need a plan. Fast."

Grandma Murray finally emerged from the school and started the car. Throughout the drive, Jared and Lenny ran plans past the eight ball.

Fake delivery?

SECURITY CAMERAS

Sneak in through a basement window?

ALARM SYSTEM

Chimney?

YOU'RE NOT SANTA

Sewer?

GROSS

By the time they reached Lakeview Drive, they

were no closer to a plan than they were when they left. Also more bad news: the houses at the end of the street were all behind a tall gate with bars that ended in spiky points at the top. It was a fancy gate with one of those electric card readers. Grandma Murray parked on the street. "Now what?" she asked.

Jared had no idea. The van was silent for a few seconds as everyone stared at the lake. "Look out there." Lenny pointed at clouds rolling in. "It's getting real dark."

That's when Jared remembered one of the very first questions he'd asked the eight ball. He asked it again. "What will the weather be today?"

PARTLY SUNNY WITH A STRONG THUNDERSTORM AT 3:10 P.M.

Jared smiled. "I've got an idea." He hopped out of the van, ran to the front and snapped off the antennae. Grandma Murray gasped.

"No time to explain, sorry Mrs. Murray!" Jared said. He sprinted down the street while yelling questions at the eight ball.

Lenny finally caught up to him. "What in the world are you doing?!"

"Making a lightning rod."

"A what?!"

Instead of replying, Jared jumped onto a low-hanging branch of a nearby tree and began climbing. The first drops of rain started falling. He climbed high enough to look down on the houses, glanced at his eight ball for a second, then picked an old-looking branch to climb onto. Even though the branch bent beneath his weight, he pressed forward. Finally, when it looked impossible for the branch to sag this much without snapping, Jared stopped and aimed the antennae like a spear. He glanced back at the eight ball, adjusted his aim a little, then cocked the antennae behind his head and launched it at a downward diagonal angle. The antennae flew through the air and...

ZAP!

...Stuck in the coils next to the trash-can-looking transformer thing on top of a nearby telephone pole. The coils sparked a little bit, but nothing else happened. The antennae remained sticking straight up in the air. Jared admired his work for a second before climbing back down and dropping next to Lenny. "Back to the van!"

Wind started whipping around them and the rain fell harder as the cousins sprinted to the van. The dark clouds had rolled overhead now, making it feel like nighttime. It got so dark that the streetlights came on. After hopping inside the van and slamming the door, Lenny turned to Jared. "You want to tell me what's going on yet?"

"You'll see."

"When?!"

"In five, four, three, two, one." Jared pointed to his telephone pole lightning rod. Just then a gigantic lightning bolt struck it and the loudest clap of thunder that Jared had ever heard shook the van. The transformer on top of the telephone pole exploded, and all the streetlights went dark.

"Come on," Jared said as he opened the door. Lenny followed him out.

"Where are you going?" Grandma Murray called after them. "How can I help?"

"We're getting Bre now," Jared said. "We need you to stay here so you can drive her to the hospital."

Lenny caught up to Jared and pushed open the now unlocked gate. The cousins found house number 14346 — the tall, old house at the end of the street — and started running. "Where is Bre?" Jared asked.

SECOND LEVEL, THIRD WINDOW FROM THE LEFT

Jared looked up. No easy way to get there.

"Where are the bad guys?"

GETTING FLASHLIGHTS IN THE BASEMENT

Jared grabbed a handful of gravel and ran to a tree near the house. He climbed up to the same level as Bre's window and looked in. Even though the room was dark, he could make out the outline of a shaking girl. He threw the gravel. Bre half turned. He threw more gravel. She came to the window.

Jared gasped when he saw her face. It was red and blotchy and beyond puffy. He signaled for her to open the window. She shook her head "no." He pointed to the eight ball and mouthed, "It's OK." She finally, shakily cracked open the window, all the while cringing as if she expected a security alarm to go off. Jared held up the EpiPen and signaled for Bre to open the window more. She nodded and weakly creaked the window open a few more inches. As she did, Jared sized up his opportunity.

The tree was about 15 yards away from the house, and Bre had only been able to open the window about eight inches. With the wind whipping around him, the throw seemed impossible. "How can I make this work?" Jared asked the eight ball.

BEES

"Bees? Bees?! WHAT DOES THAT MEAN?"

REPLY HAZY, TRY AGAIN

Jared felt a stab of fear in his heart. No! Nononono, the 24-hour timer couldn't be up already! "Please tell me how I can make this throw!"

MOST LIKELY

"Please!"

YOU MAY RELY ON IT

"Hey," Lenny shouted up. "I forgot to let you know earlier, but it's 3:30! Is that important?"

Jared had run out of time and options. Dr. Plotke would be back in Bre's room any second now, and yelling at the no-longer-magic eight ball was just wasting time. He took a deep breath, aimed the EpiPen and launched it toward Bre's window with all his might.

The throw looked all wrong coming out of Jared's hand. It was way too high and far to the left. But as the pen flipped through the air, a miraculous gust of wind caught hold of it and blew it back toward the window. It was still going to fall just short, but Bre used the last of her strength to lunge for the window and catch the pen before it could clatter off the house and fall to the ground.

YES! Jared collapsed onto his branch and gave Lenny a thumbs up. Bre took a moment to collect herself, then pulled the EpiPen inside and fumbled with the cap. Her hands were shaking so badly that she needed ten seconds and all her effort just to remove the cap.

"Come on, come on, come on," Jared mouthed.

Bre revealed the needle underneath the cap and brought it to her skin to stick herself. As she did, another lightning strike and roll of thunder startled her into dropping the pen. When she bent down to pick it up, Jared saw the door behind her swing open and a blinding flashlight beam appear.

Dr. Plotke.

Bre dove onto the EpiPen, but it was too late. Dr. Plotke ran over, threw her aside and picked up the pen. He turned it over in his hand a few times, then snapped it in half. He then swept the flashlight out the window to illuminate Jared in the tree.

CHAPTER SEVENTEEN
BEN FRANKLIN'S KITE

For the third time in the last three hours, Jared found himself being marched into a small room. This time, Lenny got the privilege of joining him.

After Dr. Plotke had found him with the flashlight, Jared yelled a warning to Lenny and tried to scramble to the ground. Too late. Burly Greg was there in a flash and intercepted the cousins before they could run for help. Now Greg was marching them into Bre's room, where they'd have to watch their friend suffer.

Once inside the room, Greg shoved Lenny to Dr. Plotke, who grabbed him by the collar. Dr. Plotke looked Lenny up and down. "Are you interested in science, young man?"

"She needs help!" Lenny yelled.

By this point, Bre had curled into a ball in the corner and was shaking uncontrollably.

"Her body is helping itself," Dr. Plotke said. He turned to Bre and smiled. "You're watching history here. It's like standing with Ben Franklin as he flew the kite."

"You gotta see that this isn't working!" Lenny yelled. "Please, she only has a few minutes left."

"Oh I'm sorry, but you're the one who only has a few minutes left," Dr. Plotke said.

Jared's mind was racing. He knew they still had one last, small hope, but they'd need some sort of distraction, and they'd need it quick. That's when he remembered the eight ball's last message. With nothing else to go on, he waved to get Lenny's attention. When Lenny finally looked over, he mouthed the eight ball's one-word message.

"Bees."

Lenny cocked his head.

"Bees," Jared mouthed again more dramatically.

"Fleas?" Lenny mouthed back. He was the worst at reading lips.

Dr. Plotke was done fooling around. He nodded to Greg. Greg reached for the gun on his side. Out of time. Jared grabbed the eight ball from his pocket and hurled it at Dr. Plotke. Bullseye! It smashed into the doctor's forehead directly between his eyes. As

Dr. Plotke stumbled backward, his lab coat flapped open, revealing the jar of bees he kept with him at all times.

"Bees! Lenny yelped as he finally understood. He lunged for the jar and threw it to Jared. Of course, Lenny being Lenny, the jar fell well short of its mark and shattered on the ground. The bees took advantage of their newfound freedom by furiously trying to sting everything in sight.

"AHHHHHHH!"

Someone in the room let out an ear-piercing scream. Jared looked around confused.

"AHHHHHHH! GET THEM AWAY!"

It was Greg. Big, burly Greg screaming like a little girl.

"ALLERGIC! I'M ALLERGIC TO BEES!"

Greg sprinted out of the room. Dr. Plotke rubbed his head. "GREG! GREG, GET BACK HERE!"

"AHHHHHH!" They heard Greg continue to scream downstairs. Then they heard a different voice.

"Come out with your hands up!"

Jared, Lenny and Dr. Plotke all ran to the window. It was Vice Principal Fuqua holding a bullhorn. He was surrounded by a half dozen police trying to take their bullhorn back. Mr. Fuqua ducked and dodged and locked eyes with Jared.

"Come out with your hands up!"

CHAPTER EIGHTEEN
BE SUPER

After the arrests, after the paramedics, after the news crews, after Vice Principal Fuqua's unsuccessful fifth attempt to get the cousins hauled off in handcuffs, Jared and Lenny found themselves alone in the back of Jared's mom's minivan.

"I'm told this belongs to you?" A police officer stuck his head into the window and held out the iPod Jared had given to Kodey.

"Yes! Thank you!" Jared grabbed the iPod and smiled.

Lenny squinched his eyes at the iPod. "But didn't... I thought... OK, what just happened?"

"Kodey Kline and Mr. Fuqua just saved our lives."

"I don't get it."

"I was real nervous about not having a plan this afternoon. But when Kodey showed up, I realized that he could be the perfect emergency backup in case we couldn't help Bre on our own."

"But how?"

"This." Jared held out the iPod. "As I was handing it to him, I set an alarm to go off right around the time that the magic eight ball would run out. That also happened to be the same time Kodey would be serving his after-school detention for our little scuffle this morning. Since electronics aren't supposed to be in detention, I figured the teacher would confiscate the iPod once it started beeping. I left a little message in the alarm description for her. Look."

JARED AND LENNY AT 14346 LAKEVIEW DRIVE. BRING POLICE AND AMBULANCE.

"Wow!" Lenny said. "You really are a superhero!"

"A superhero? You think you're a superhero now?" Jared's mom stepped into the car, red-faced. "Is that why you felt like you could lie about the library last night?"

Uh oh.

"Is that why you got in a fight today? Is that why you faked a teacher's note?" She was just warming up. "Is that why you ran away from school? Is that why you vandalized the vice principal's office? You will buy that man a new poster, by the way. Is that why you..."

Jared slumped in his seat.

After telling his parents the whole story, Jared negotiated his grounding down to a month. They understood that he was helping a friend (even though they still didn't quite buy the whole magic eight ball thing), and he understood that he'd made a whole lot of mistakes along the way.

In addition to the grounding at home, Jared also had to serve a month of after-school detentions. Jared knew that, although a month of after-school detentions is no fun, his punishment was a lot less severe than Grandma Murray's. She cooperated with police to put Dr. Plotke and his gang away for a long time, but helping someone mess with kids' food is still a serious crime.

As Jared walked to his locker before his final after-school detention, he heard a *psst* in the hallway. It was Breanna Burris grinning a giant grin. Bre had been released from the hospital two weeks ago. The doctor who treated her said that he'd never seen someone get an allergic reaction that bad, for that long and survive to tell about it. He estimated that if she went just a few more minutes without help, she wouldn't have made it. Of course she had to be extra careful now, because she was more allergic to wheat than ever (much to Dr. Plotke's surprise).

Jared walked over. "Need some help getting rid of those cookies?"

Over the last month, Bre had become a star at school. People were still giving her cards and stuffed animals and plates of gluten-free cookies. She was holding such a plate right now.

"Oh uh, no, but you can have one!"

Jared took one. It tasted like cardboard stuffed with chocolate chips. He tried to smile as he chewed.

Bre pulled him aside, shoved something in his face and lowered her voice. "Look!"

It was a note written with perfect handwriting on a single sheet of notebook paper.

TOMORROW. 8 A.M. ELEMENTARY SCHOOL PLAYGROUND. GET READY TO BE SUPER.

Jared's eyes got wide. "Wait, you're not doing it are you? After everything that happened?"

"You shouldn't talk with your mouth full," Bre said.

Jared swallowed the last of the crumbly cookie. "I mean, you just…"

"Relax," Bre said. "It's what I do." She winked and practically skipped away.

Jared shook his head and walked to his own locker. When he opened it, a single sheet of notebook paper fluttered to the ground. He picked it up. The note contained only two words written in perfect handwriting.

YOU TOO.

SNEAK PEEK
TRAPPED IN A VIDEO GAME

Continue the story in **Superhero for a Day Book Two**, *coming November 2016. To find out how you can get the first chapter for free before anyone else, visit* **dustinbradybooks.com.** *In the meantime, check out the first chapter of Dustin Brady's other series* — **Trapped in a Video Game** — *available now on Amazon.com.*

Jesse. Come over. Now. You're not going to believe this.

That was the text that ruined my life.

I know I know, that doesn't sound like a life ruiner. Especially because the text's sender, my friend Eric, says "you're not going to believe this" about the world's most believable things. Just in the last month, he's told me that I wouldn't believe a piece of toast that looked "exactly like Darth Vader" (it looked exactly like a burnt piece of toast), a sweet trick he learned on his bike (riding for literally one half of one second without holding onto the handlebars) and a really big booger (that one actually was pretty impressive).

I ignored the text for a little bit, because nothing makes Eric talk faster than silence. When he didn't write back after five minutes, I finally replied.

What is it?

No response.

You gonna tell me or what?

Nothing.

This better not be another booger.

Nope.

Five more minutes went by. I sighed. Fine, Eric was going to win this one. But only because looking at his dumb booger would be more fun than this math homework. I closed my book, put on my jacket and walked across the street to Eric's house.

The door was open, so I let myself in and walked down to the basement. "All right, let's see it," I said as I reached the bottom of the stairs.

No booger. Also no Eric.

"Come on," I called out. I wandered into the laundry room (where the dirty clothes should be). I walked upstairs into Eric's room (where the dirty clothes actually were). I checked behind all the doors, inside all the closets and under all the beds. No booger. No Eric.

I couldn't believe it.

Ever since Eric's family moved into the house across the street from mine in first grade, his favorite activity has been playing practical jokes on me. I appreciate a good practical joke as much as the next guy; unfortunately, none of Eric's practical jokes are good. Because he's so impatient, he ruins every joke before it even begins. I don't know how many sleepovers I've been to where Eric has attempted to dip a sleeping friend's finger in warm water, only to have the water dumped over his head by the "victim" who'd had his eyes closed for less than 30 seconds.

So on one hand, I had to admire Eric's commitment to this particular joke. On the other, it may have been his dumbest yet.

Back in the basement, I decided that I'd had enough. "OK!" I yelled to an empty house. "I'm going back home now! I have to finish the math homework due Monday! Maybe you should do the same!"

More silence. I looked around. The only sign of life anywhere was a video game paused on the TV in the corner. Eric loved his video games. Especially the one on the screen right now — Full Blast. Never heard of Full Blast? That's because it's not out yet. Eric got it two weeks ago from Charlie, the coolest kid in our class. To clarify — Charlie isn't the coolest kid in sixth grade because he's actually a cool kid. He's the coolest because his dad works for a video game company and sometimes gives Charlie's friends early copies of games to test.

For the last two weeks, Eric's mouth has been going full blast about Full Blast.

"Jesse, I'm telling you. It is the greatest video game ever made!"

"I don't care."

"All these aliens are trying to take over the world, and you're the only person alive who can save everyone, because…"

"I don't care."

"Because you found one of their blasters, and once you charge it to FULL BLAST you can…"

"I DON'T CARE!"

"You can start shooting…"

Eric never stopped trying to get me to watch him play his new game. I never went because I would rather get sprayed in the face with a fire hose full blast than watch someone else play video games. I don't hate video games — I'm sure they're fine. I've just never really had time to sit down and play them.

I walked toward the TV. I'd never heard Eric rant about a game like he ranted about this one. Maybe I should give it a chance. At the very least, it would probably beat math homework. I picked up the controller and looked at the screen.

ARE YOU SURE?

- YES

- NO

I paused for a second. Should I? What if I erased Eric's saved game? Nah, he wouldn't mind. He'd just be happy I was trying a video game. I clicked **YES**.

The instant I did everything went black. Not everything on the screen. Everything in *the room.*

Find out what happens next in **Trapped in a Video Game: Book One**, *available now.*

A NOTE FROM THE AUTHOR

Hey! Thanks for taking the time to read *Superhero for a Day: The Magic Magic Eight Ball*. I hope you had as much fun reading it as I had writing it. If you liked it, please consider telling your friends or posting a short review on Amazon. Word of mouth is an author's best friend and much appreciated.

If you want to get in touch with me, I'd love to hear from you! You can email me at any time at dustin@dustinbradybooks.com.

Thanks again for reading my book!

ABOUT THE AUTHOR
DUSTIN BRADY

Dustin Brady lives in Cleveland, Ohio with his wife, Deserae, and puppy, Nugget. Every day he wakes up thinking that maybe today will finally be the day that he gets bitten by a radioactive spider.

ABOUT THE ILLUSTRATOR
JESSE BRADY

Jesse Brady is a professional illustrator and animator in Pensacola, Florida. His superpower is the ability to burp the Spider-Man theme song all the way through.

Made in the USA
San Bernardino, CA
08 September 2018